13.95

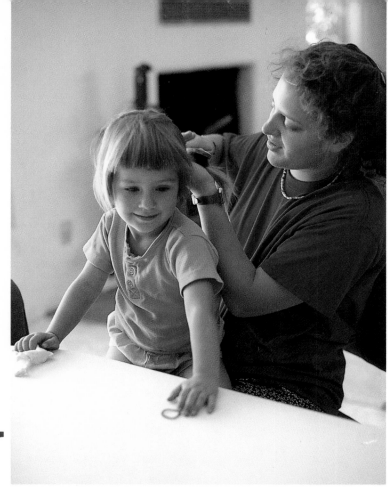

My
New
Baby-Sitter

BY CHRISTINE LOOMIS

PHOTOGRAPHS BY GEORGE ANCONA

MORROW JUNIOR BOOKS / NEW YORK

To Bill, Kira, and Molly,
and to baby-sitters everywhere
who give love and care to children
and peace of mind to parents
C. L.

To Rosemary Brosnan
G. A.

Thanks to the people who took part in the
photography of the book:
Helga, Isabel and Marina Ancona
Nikolai J. Armendariz
Tanya Barfield
Mary and Shari Beacham
Mariko Cohen
Gwen H. Delgado
Isa Fox
Stephanie Gonzales
Krista Hughes
La Wanda Johnson
Damu King
Zane Maroney
Amelia and Ruthe Morand
Carlos and Carlos Jesus Quiñones
Brandi and Kathie Romero
Aileen N. Sie

The text type is 14 point Century Book.

1 2 3 4 5 6 7 8 9 10

Library of Congress Cataloging-in-Publication Data. Loomis, Christine. My new baby-sitter / Christine Loomis ; photographs by George Ancona.
p.   cm. Summary: Explores real-life caregiving situations with reassurance and insight in a story for children, and a "Note to Parents" offers essential advice about how to choose a caregiver. ISBN 0-688-09625-5.—ISBN 0-688-09626-3 (lib. bdg.).
1. Babysitting—Juvenile literature. [1. Babysitters.] I. Ancona, George, ill. II. Title.
HQ769.5.L66 1991 649′.1′0248—dc20 90-38527 CIP AC

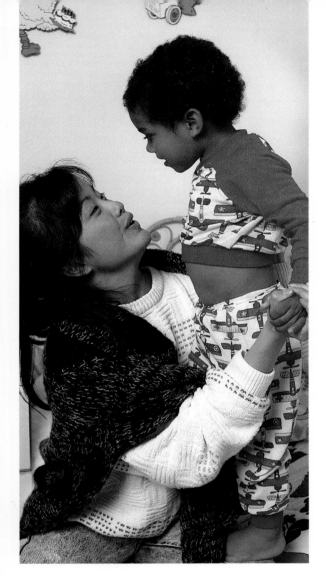

Note
to
Parents

A new caregiver is an important
addition to any family. It will take time for
every family member to develop a solid,
trusting relationship with her, but it will be
time well spent, for an excellent caregiver
offers parents much more than a few hours
off from childcare. She can help reduce
family feelings of stress or anxiety, be
another source of affection and support for
children, and give parents peace of mind by
allowing them to go out secure in the
knowledge that their children are well
cared for. (Because most caregivers are
women, they are referred to as "she" in this
book.)

Leaving your children with a new sitter
can be especially challenging: Children
crave routine and consistency. There are
ways to ease this transition period,
however, and to get the relationship off to
the best possible start. What you do will
depend in part on the ages of your children
and on what kind of care you have—live-in,
live-out, family daycare, an occasional
evening sitter, a foreign au pair, or a mix of

several options. Remember: There is no one right way to do things, no one right answer. Use these suggestions as a guide, adapting them to your family and child-rearing style.

Before the Sitter Arrives

Talk to your children about why your family needs a baby-sitter. If you are going to work for the first time, discuss why you are doing so. If possible, take your child to where you will be working. Having a mental picture of where a parent is during the day helps some children cope better.

If you're going out for the evening, explain where you are going and that Mommy and Daddy need special time together, too. Don't minimize children's anxieties about your leaving. While the fact that you will be gone only a few hours may seem inconsequential to you, it can seem like a long time to very young children. Their anxiety is an emotional response, not a rational process, so telling them to "be reasonable" or suggesting that their anxiety is "silly" will not change how they feel. Just be as reassuring and straightforward as possible. Explain that you will be back and when. And, although it may be tempting to avoid an emotional scene at the door as you leave, *never* sneak out without letting your child know you are going. Doing so

will only make your child more dependent, more clingy, and more fearful of your leaving.

If you are looking for a full-time sitter, involving your child in the hiring process can help ease his or her adjustment, too. Older children can, for example, make a list of their own interview questions to ask prospective caregivers. After they do so, they may have definite opinions about why they do or do not like certain applicants. Listen to their concerns. Younger children may not be as articulate; however, their presence at an interview allows you to see firsthand how a caregiver interacts with children of that age. It's not unusual for a baby-sitter to be better with one age than another. Even an infant can help you. You can watch how a prospective caregiver handles the baby at an interview. Is she comfortable? Does she smile? How does the baby respond? Infants need vocal and visual stimulation, cuddling, and eye contact with the significant adults in their lives. A sitter who doesn't provide this is not a good caregiver for infants.

If you're planning to use family daycare, take your child to the homes of several daycare providers. Watch how the sitter interacts with the children there. How does your child fit into the group? How does the provider's "style" with children mesh with your own and with your child's personality? And is the caregiver licensed by your state? Ask for other parents as references.

Whether you opt for full-time, part-time, in-home, or family daycare, the bottom line is to find someone who really does care, for whom this will be more than just a job. Technique is secondary to a caregiver's ability to be compassionate and empathic with children.

You've Found a Great Caregiver

Once you've decided on the right person for your family, ease into it. If you hire an in-home sitter, have her come for a few hours a day for at least a couple of days when you can be there, too. If you're getting a live-in nanny or au pair from far away, arrange for her to arrive on a weekend, when you can be home. If your choice is family daycare, plan to stay with your child at the caregiver's home the first few times. Once you and your child are comfortable with that, you can drop your child off at the house for short periods, gradually building up to a full day. And drop in yourself over the next few weeks, whether at your home or your sitter's. This allows your child and caregiver time alone, but it also reassures your child that even though you leave, you will return.

As you spend time with your caregiver in this initial period, you have the chance to make sure that she understands and is respecting your child-rearing practices and beliefs, regardless of how *she* was raised or how she raises her own children. For example, if you don't believe in spanking, you don't want a sitter who uses hitting as a means of discipline; if you don't want your child watching a lot of television, your sitter should not count on plopping the kids in front of the TV while she does something else. Dropping in and out should give you firsthand knowledge of how the sitter approaches some of these issues. And encourage your children to talk to you about their time with the baby-sitter. If, by chance, anything is awry, you don't want your children to feel afraid to tell you.

Of course, communication with your caregiver is equally important. The more she knows about you and your family, the more consistent your child's care will be. Tell her about any quirks or fears your child may have—fear of the dark, a dislike of certain foods, a need for a security object at nap or bedtime. And be specific about other things: how many sweets your child can have, when nap or bedtime is, and so on. Remember, your caregiver can't read your mind.

You may not think of everything, so it is also a good idea to tell your caregiver that if she and your child disagree on how something should be done, she should call you. If she can't reach you, she should go along with your child (unless, of course, doing so would put your child's health or safety at risk) and talk to you about it at the end of the day. This can prevent unnecessary battles between your child and caregiver and keep your child from feeling that he or she is powerless if you are not there.

In addition, let your children know that if they want to call you, they can. If you can't receive calls, tell your child that you will call on your break or at lunch, and then be sure to call. And *always* tell your children that no one—not even their baby-sitter—should ever ask them to keep a secret from Mommy and Daddy.

Finally, whichever form of childcare you use, and however experienced your caregiver is, always give her *written* information to be used in case of an emergency. Your sitter should have a telephone number for you, for your spouse, and for your pediatrician, as well as any pertinent emergency numbers, such as an ambulance service, the nearest hospital, and the number of the local poison-control center. Post these numbers near your phone at home or keep them in the bag your child will be taking to the sitter's house each day. And don't forget to include a signed medical-release form so that medical care for your child will not be delayed if you cannot be reached.

Activities and Ideas

No matter how wonderful a sitter is, you can't expect her to be a child-development expert. Do some research yourself to find out which toys are appropriate for your child's age; what developmental stages your child is likely to go through in the next few months; what kinds of activities will reinforce or augment your child's development. Share this information with your caregiver and discuss different ways to use it.

Naturally, you can't orchestrate every moment that your child and caregiver spend together, nor should you want to. Don't be afraid to let your sitter use her own unique abilities. Sitters from foreign countries or even different areas of this country can offer your child stories, ideas, games, and more that you might not be able to. Encourage your child and caregiver to develop their own special relationship. They will both benefit from it. And don't worry that by doing so you will become less important in your child's life. No matter how wonderful the sitter, no matter how close your child grows to her, no sitter will ever replace you in your child's eyes and heart.

When a Sitter Leaves

Changing caregivers can be a difficult time for your family. Try to arrange transitions at times when you or your spouse can be there to spend more time with your child. Keep in mind that children sometimes think their bad behavior has caused a sitter to leave, or that a baby-sitter doesn't care about them anymore and that's why she's leaving. You and the caregiver should assure your children that this is not the case. Even if your baby-sitter is leaving on less than great terms with you, your children may still see her as a cherished friend. Ask your caregiver to let your children know that she still cares about them and that they can write or call her.

Try to arrange occasional contact, too, especially right after the sitter leaves. This can help make future transitions easier. And take the time to let a new caregiver know of your child's attachment to the previous sitter. She needs to be especially patient and understanding, and to recognize that a young child may be angry at her for replacing the old sitter. This can be hard on a new caregiver, so remember that she needs your support and understanding as much as your child does.

As Time Goes By

Even as things move along smoothly with your caregiver, you need to take action to see that all continues to go well. Talk to your sitter about her work on a regular basis. Talk to your child every day. Pick a relaxed time—not five minutes before dinner is ready—so you won't feel rushed. And listen to your child. Some children have a resistance to going to a sitter or to being left, but continued or heightened opposition may signal a deeper problem.

Of course, even small problems need attention. Assure your child and your caregiver that you will work to resolve them. Don't make assumptions about who is right and who is wrong, and avoid blaming either party. The important thing is to let your child *and* your caregiver know that you support them both and that speaking up about a problem is the right thing to do. And remember, like any relationship, the relationship between your caregiver and your family is one that takes work. However, a good relationship will be rewarding and wonderful for all of you.

7

Are you getting a baby-sitter? Some of your friends probably have a baby-sitter, too. Lots of children do.

A baby-sitter is someone who takes care of you when your mom and dad have someplace to go. If they go to work or lunch or a meeting, a baby-sitter will take care of you in the daytime. If they go out to dinner or a movie, they will find someone to watch you at night. That way, even when your parents can't be with you, they know you are okay.

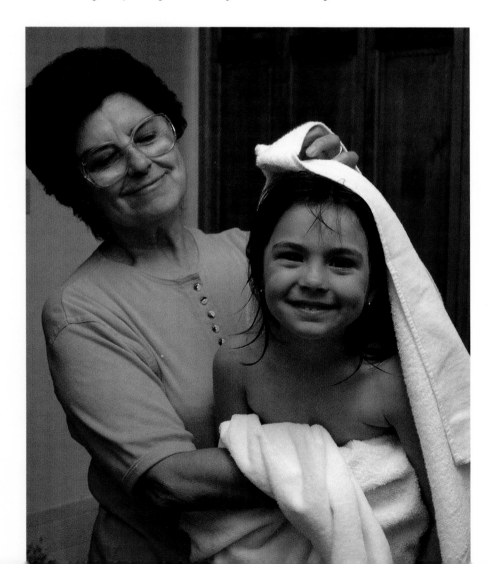

Being with a baby-sitter isn't very different from being with Mommy and Daddy. You can do all of the same things. Baby-sitters can help you get dressed, color pictures, read stories, make lunch, and take you to the park.

What's your favorite thing to do? Your baby-sitter will probably be able to do that with you.

The first time you stay with a baby-sitter, you might feel sad because you miss your mommy and daddy.

The first time Gracie stayed with Tara, Gracie was mad at her mom and dad for leaving her. And she was worried that they wouldn't come back. Now Gracie doesn't worry. She knows her parents will always come back.

What if you don't like your baby-sitter? That can happen sometimes.

Tommy used to go to Jean's house, but he was unhappy there because Jean made him drink milk. Tommy hates milk, but Jean said he had to drink it at her house. At first, Tommy was afraid to tell his parents about it because he thought they would be mad at him. When Tommy finally told his mom and dad, they weren't mad at him at all. They said Tommy didn't have to go back to Jean's house.

It isn't always easy to tell your mom and dad how you feel. But if you don't let them know when you are unhappy, they can't help you feel better.

Your baby-sitter can be one of your best friends. If she takes care of you for a long time, she may even seem like part of your family. That's a nice feeling.

Sometimes, though, baby-sitters move away or even change jobs. Tara did. Before she started taking care of Gracie, Tara took care of another little girl in a different town. Tara still thinks about her. They send each other funny cards.

If your baby-sitter leaves someday, you can always write or call each other. Getting letters and calls from an old friend is a nice feeling, too.

In the Daytime

Gracie's mother is going to start a new job, so Gracie needs someone to take care of her during the day. But Gracie didn't want a baby-sitter. "Why do you have to go to work?" she asked.

Gracie's mother pulled her up on her lap and gave her a big hug. "I'm going to work to help take care of our family, just like Daddy does. I'll miss being with you during the day, but I'll still love you as much as I do now. And I promise we'll find someone wonderful to take care of you."

It can take a while to find just the right person to take care of you. Gracie's mom talked on the phone to lots and lots of people who wanted to be Gracie's baby-sitter. She asked them questions and they answered. They asked her questions, too. That's called an interview.

If Gracie's mother liked someone on the phone, she asked them to come to the house to meet Gracie. Then Gracie helped with the interview. First, there was Samantha. Samantha didn't smile much, and she told Gracie to mind her manners and not to interrupt. Gracie and her mother were glad when Samantha left.

Sally was nice, but she smoked cigarettes and Gracie thought she smelled bad.

Finally, Tara called. And when Tara came to the house, she smiled a lot. She said, "Gracie, I'd like to be your friend. Will you be my friend?"

Gracie likes the idea of a new friend. She likes Tara.

Today is the first day Tara will stay alone with Gracie all day. Even though Gracie likes Tara, she will still miss Mommy.

Gracie's mom gives Gracie a piece of paper with her telephone number at work on it. "Call me whenever you want to," she tells Gracie.

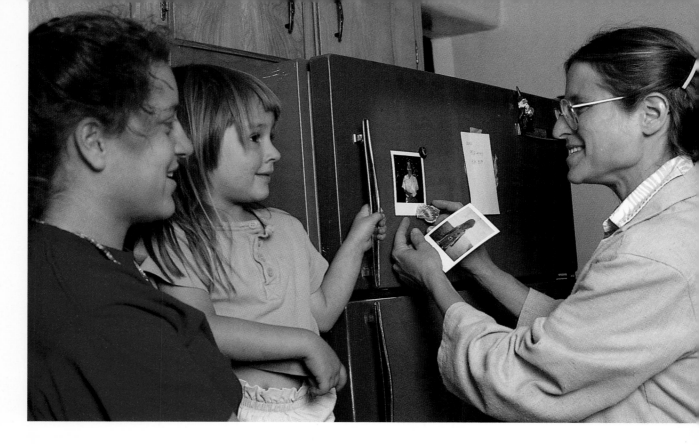

Gracie's mother has something else, too. She shows Gracie two photographs. "I'm going to take this picture of you to my new office," she says, "so I can see you all day. That will help me not to miss you so much. And you can have this picture of me to keep with you."

Gracie puts Mommy's picture on the refrigerator, where she can look at it whenever she wants to.

You can ask your mom and dad for a picture, too. Don't forget to give them one of you.

19

After Gracie's mom leaves, Tara has a surprise. "I was the best bubble-blower on my street when I was your age," Tara says. She shows Gracie how to blow great big bubbles. Gracie isn't so sad now.

"Will you play hide-and-seek with me?" Gracie asks. "Okay," Tara says. "I'll be 'it.'" Tara counts to twenty.

Soon it's snack time. Tara makes apple slices with peanut butter. Gracie makes designs with them on her plate.

"What should we do now?" Tara asks. "It's your turn to think of something." Gracie decides on dress-up. She gets out a big bag of dress-up clothes. Gracie puts on her big-lady necklace and hat. She gives Tara a funny hat. Gracie pretends she is the teacher and Tara is the little girl. Tara makes a sad face.

"It's all right, little girl," Gracie tells Tara. "Your mother will be back soon." Gracie hugs Tara, and that makes them both feel better.

Gracie helps Tara make lunch. They pretend they
are hiding from wild animals and eat under the table.

Soon Gracie is feeling a little sleepy. It's nap time. Tara gives Gracie a piggyback ride to bed. She tucks her in and pulls down the shades. "Don't close the door all the way," Gracie reminds her. Tara tiptoes out and leaves the door open just the way Gracie likes it.

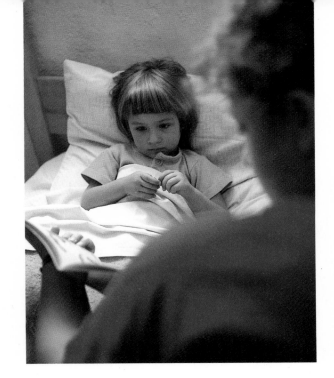

When Gracie wakes up from her nap, she calls for Mommy. When Tara comes instead, Gracie cries. She forgot her mother wasn't there. Tara has an idea. "Why don't you call your mom? I'll help you dial."

As soon as Gracie hears her mother's voice, she feels much better. Have you ever talked to your mom or dad on the telephone?

It's a nice afternoon, so Gracie and Tara go to the playground in the park. Lots of other children are there with their baby-sitters.

There's Gracie's friend Lauren. Her baby-sitter is Ashi and she's from Jamaica. That's an island. Ashi picks Lauren up from nursery school every day. Sometimes Lauren's mom and dad go away for a weekend. Then Lauren has her own vacation. She spends the weekend at Ashi's house. Ashi says Lauren is her favorite guest.

There are some baby-sitters who live with the children they take care of—even at night. A baby-sitter who lives with a family is called a nanny or an au pair. That's a French word. Gracie's friend Lucie has a nanny, but she's not French. She's from Wisconsin. Lucie says having a nanny is like having a big sister.

Afternoon is a good time for errands. Lauren and Ashi have laundry to do. Lauren likes to help measure the detergent. Then Ashi lets her put the quarters in to start the machine: one, two, three, four quarters.

Your baby-sitter might take you to the grocery store or the cleaners or the bank. You might walk or take a bus. Or you might go in the car. Which would you rather do?

It's almost five o'clock. Gracie waits by the window for her mom. When she comes home, she and Gracie share a big hug. They're glad to see each other. "Now you tell me all about your day and I'll tell you all about mine," says Gracie's mom. Gracie gets comfortable. She has a lot to tell.

When your mom and dad get home, you'll have a lot to tell them, too.

Not all baby-sitters will come to your house.
Phyllis stays in her house, and the children she takes
care of come to her. That's called family daycare, and
Phyllis is called a caregiver.

Every morning, Tommy and his father drive to
Phyllis's house. There are four other children who go
there, too. Tommy has no brothers or sisters, so he
likes having friends to play with every day.

It's eight o'clock when Tommy arrives at Phyllis's house. The other children are arriving, too. Phyllis takes everyone to the backyard to play. She has a swing set, a sandbox, a jungle gym, and lots of toys. Tommy likes to hang by his knees from the jungle gym. Can you do that?

Today, some of the children are building a castle out of blocks. Daniel fits inside. Tommy and Hannah are using crayons. Tommy makes a drawing for his dad. Hannah makes a drawing for her dad. You can make a picture for Daddy or Mommy, too. What will you draw?

Soon it's time for lunch. Tommy is glad. He thinks Phyllis is a good cook.

After lunch, it's story time. All the children get out blue mats to sit on. Phyllis reads a story, and when it's over, the children lie down on their mats. Tommy tries hard not to fall asleep, but he does.

At the end of a busy day, Phyllis puts a record on the record player. There's time to play "London Bridge Is Falling Down" one more time. Then Tommy's dad and the other parents are there to pick up their children. Tommy shows his dad the picture he made. "I love it," his father says. "I'm going to hang it up at work."

Everyone is ready to go home now. "Good-bye, Phyllis. See you in the morning!"

At Night

Parents like to go out at night sometimes. They may eat dinner in a restaurant, or see a movie or a play in a theater, or visit friends, just like you do. When your mom and dad go out, they will call a baby-sitter to come take care of you for a few hours. They may call the same one every time, or they may call different ones.

Some baby-sitters are young. Susan is in high school. Bonnie is a grandmother, but she's a baby-sitter, too.

When your mom and dad go out at night, they may come back before you go to bed. Or they may not come back until after you've fallen asleep.

Matthew's mother and father are going to a movie, so Susan is coming to stay with him. Matthew doesn't know Susan. He wants his mom and dad to stay home.

Matthew's dad understands. "When I was a little boy, I didn't want my mom and dad to go out, either," he tells Matthew.

"Did they stay home?"

"No," Matthew's dad says, "they didn't. But they let me make a list of important things to tell the baby-sitter so she'd know just how to take care of me. Would you like to do that?"

Matthew tells his dad just what to put on the list.

Matthew's parents will be home before he falls asleep. They promise. But even that seems like a long time to Matthew.

When Susan comes, Matthew's parents talk to Susan about all of the important things on their list: dinner, where they can be reached, and when Matthew should get ready for bed. Now it's time for them to go.

Matthew holds on to his mom.

"Go and get *your* list," she tells him, "so Susan will know which story to read later."

Matthew gets two good-bye kisses: one from his mom and one from his dad. Then he gets his list and gives it to Susan. It says:

Don't touch Henry
No broccoli
Goggles
Lights on for bed
Read *Curious George*
One special treat
No hugs, no kisses

You can make a list for your baby-sitter. What will you put on it?

"This is a good list," Susan tells Matthew. "But who is Henry?"

Matthew gets Henry from his bed. He's a very special bear. "I won't touch him," Susan promises. "But maybe he will want to play with us later."

Matthew doesn't think so.

For dinner, Susan makes her super-duper hamburger and no broccoli. "I don't like broccoli, either," she says. Then she asks Matthew if Henry wants to join them for dinner. "No," says Matthew, "he doesn't."

After dinner, Susan gives Matthew a chocolate cupcake and a note. It says "One Special Treat. Love, Mommy."

What would your special treat be?

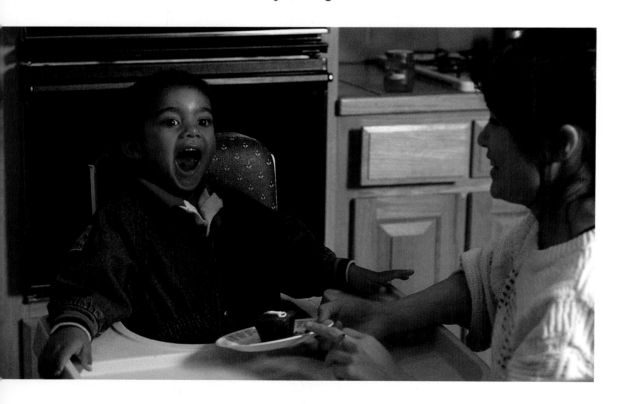

It's bath time. Matthew puts his duck, tugboat, ball, and hippopotamus family in the tub with him. What a crowd!

When it's time for Susan to wash his hair, she puts swimming goggles on him so the shampoo won't get in his eyes. She says Matthew looks like a frogman. Matthew says, "Ribbit."

Maybe Matthew is beginning to like Susan just a little.

Susan helps Matthew brush his teeth. She makes funny faces in the mirror. Matthew makes funny faces, too. "Henry can make funny faces when he wants to," says Matthew.

"I'd like to see that sometime," Susan says.

40

Once Matthew is ready for bed, it's story time.

"Do you think Henry wants to come and listen to the story?" Susan asks.

"Yes," says Matthew. "I think he does." Matthew gets Henry.

"He can sit right here next to me," Susan says. "It's nice to have a new friend. I sure hope he likes me."

"I think he does."

When Susan finishes reading *Curious George*, Matthew says, "Again." She reads it three times. Then, guess what? Mommy and Daddy are home.

"Just like we promised," says Matthew's dad.

It's time for Susan to go. "If it's okay with you and Henry, I'll come back and see you again," she tells Matthew.

Matthew smiles. "It's okay with us."

Soon he's fast asleep.

Sometimes a baby-sitter can become a special friend. Bonnie has been coming to take care of Kira and Molly for two years. Kira says Bonnie is practically a third grandma.

Tonight, Bonnie is staying until midnight. That's very late. Kira and Molly won't see their mom and dad until tomorrow morning. But Kira has a surprise for them tonight.

First, she has to have dinner. It's pizza. Kira knows how to eat neatly, but Molly makes a big mess. It's a good thing she's going to have a bath!

Kira can wash her own hair. She uses extra
shampoo and makes funny designs out of her hair.
Bonnie says she used to do the same thing when she
was a little girl. Molly likes bath time. She splashes
and splashes and gets everything all wet. Bonnie and
Kira laugh. What a mess.

It's time to get out. Bonnie wraps Kira and Molly
up in big fluffy towels and dries them off.

   After bath time, everyone gets comfortable. Bonnie
is a good storyteller. Kira likes stories about
princesses and dragons. Molly likes stories about
babies and bears. Tonight, Bonnie tells one story
about a baby princess bear, and then it's time for Kira
to work on her surprise.

   She takes some nice clean paper, some markers,
and she makes a card. It's Bonnie's idea. The card
says "Dear Mommy and Daddy. Here is a good-night
kiss from your daughter Kira. Please come give me a
good-night kiss when you come home. Love, Kira.
P.S. You can kiss Molly, too."

   She puts the card on her parents' pillow. Then it's
time for bed.

It's almost midnight. Kira and Molly are asleep.
Bonnie is reading in the living room. Soon Kira and
Molly's mom and dad are home. Bonnie tells them to
look on their pillow. They read Kira's card and tiptoe
very quietly into her room. They pull Kira's covers
snugly around her and kiss her good night. Next, they
kiss Molly. "Sweet dreams," they whisper.

Your mother and father will kiss you good night, too.
Good night. Sweet dreams. See you in the morning.